P9-APJ-341

Calamity Jane

Adapted by
Stephen Krensky

Illustrations by
Lisa Carlson

On My Own

FOLKLORE

M Millbrook Press/Minneapolis

Millbrook Press, Inc.
A division of Lerner Publishing Group
241 First Avenue North
Minneapolis, MN 55401

Website address: www.lernerbooks.com

Library of Congress Cataloging-in-Publication Data

Krensky, Stephen.
    Calamity Jane / adapted by Stephen Krensky.
       p.   cm. — (On my own folklore)
    ISBN-13: 978–1–57505–886–3 (lib. bdg. : alk. paper)
    ISBN-10: 1–57505–886–3 (lib. bdg. : alk. paper)
    1. Calamity Jane, 1852–1903 — Juvenile literature. 2. Women pioneers — West (U.S.)
       — Biography — Juvenile literature. 3. Pioneers — West (U.S.) — Biography —
    Juvenile literature. 4. West (U.S.) — Biography — Juvenile literature. I. Title.
    F594.C2K74 2007
    978.02'092—dc22   2005010185

Manufactured in the United States of America
1 2 3 4 5 6 – JR – 12 11 10 09 08 07

For my wife, Joan, who has always shown plenty of gumption
—S.K.

for Brent—first, best and always
—L.C.

Calamity Jane: A Folklore Legend

Maybe you have heard of Calamity Jane. Well, Calamity Jane is a Wild West legend. And she was a real woman by the name of Martha Jane Canary. She became an army scout and Pony Express rider. She dressed like a man because she liked to. She didn't care what other people thought about it. So it was only natural that a few exaggerations would grow up around her.

We call stories like Calamity Jane's tall tales because everything in them is extra big, extra fast, and extra wild. And the truth in these stories might be just a bit stretched. The heroes and heroines in tall tales are as tall as buildings, as strong as oxen, or as fast as lightning. They meet with wild adventures at every turn. But that's okay because they can solve just about every problem that comes their way.

Tall tales may be funny and outsized. But they describe the life that many workers and pioneers shared. The people in these stories often have jobs that real people had. And the stories are always set in familiar places.

The first tellers of these tales may have known these people and places. Or they may have wished they could be just like the hero in the story. The stories were told again and again and passed from person to person. We call such spoken and shared stories folklore.

Folklore is the stories and customs of a place or a people. Folklore can be folktales like the tall tale. These stories are usually not written down until much later, after they have been told and retold for many years. Folklore can also be sayings, jokes, and songs.

Folklore can teach us something. A rhyme or a song may help us remember an event from long ago. Or it can be just for fun, such as a good ghost story or a jump-rope song. Folklore can also tell us about the people who share the stories.

Stories about Calamity Jane are plenty wild. But there is some truth in them about life in the old West. Calamity really did come to the rescue in Deadwood. She most likely did save an army captain's life. In fact, that might be how she got her name, but it was meant as a compliment. Whenever there was a calamity around, you wanted Jane on your side.

Growing Up

Martha Jane Canary always knew
she was special.
Other girls might spend their time
playing with corn-silk dolls
or sweeping up a dirt floor.
Martha Jane was different.
She learned to ride and shoot.
And she wore clothes
that wouldn't get in her way.
She might not be in the middle
of every calamity just yet,
but she was drawn to adventure
like ants to a picnic.

One time, when Martha Jane
was playing in the Missouri woods,
she came upon a rattlesnake
sunning itself on a rock.
R-r-rattttttle went the rattlesnake,
trying to scare her.
Martha Jane just laughed.

"I'm nine years old," she said.
"And that's the most pitiful rattle
I ever did hear."
Then she opened her mouth
and let out a rattle
that was heard in three counties.
The snake was so surprised,
it died of embarrassment
right there on the spot.

When Martha Jane was 12,
her family set out with other pioneers
to move from Missouri to Montana.
They were hoping
for a better life out West.

It was a rugged five-month trip
by wagon train.
The trails were pretty rough.
Some of the ruts were so deep
that the wagon bottoms scraped
the ground as they passed by.

Whenever the wagon train came
to a river, the leader always found
a shallow place to cross.
But that didn't satisfy Martha Jane.
She looked for deeper spots
to cross over on her pony.
One time, though, she got stuck
in some quicksand
that tried to pull her under.
But Martha Jane kicked so hard
the quicksand heated up
and turned to glass.
Then she stepped out
with no trouble at all.

Every day, the men
in the wagon train went hunting.
Martha Jane wanted to go too,
but the men didn't want
to bring her along.
So she went hunting by herself.
When she returned,
she had three rabbits
slung over her shoulder.

"That's pretty good for a little squirt,"
said one of the men.
"Oh, I've got four dead deer
about a mile back,"
Martha Jane explained.
"I just couldn't carry
everything at once."

After that, the hunters were glad
for her company.

By the time the wagon train
reached Montana,

she was shooting so much game
that the pioneers had to eat
five meals a day just to keep up.

Horsing Around

Virginia City, Montana,

was a gold-mining town.

That suited Martha Jane just fine.

She poked her nose

into every nook and cranny.

"You're looking for trouble,"

some folks warned her.

"Course I am," she always replied.

"It saves time."

Miners came and went every day,
looking for new veins of gold
to make their fortune.
They were a mean bunch, for sure.
Most of them ended up
with either holes in their heads
or holes in their pockets.

But a few got lucky and struck it big.
When the shout of "Gold!" was heard,
the news traveled faster than lightning.
One miner found a nugget
the size of his fist.
Another discovered a vein of ore so rich
he wore out three shovels digging it up.

Martha Jane didn't pan much
for gold herself.
It was dull work, she thought.
Instead, she liked to stay on the move.
She had a special fondness for horses,
especially fast ones.
And she had a knack for handling them.
One time, some cowboys
brought wild horses to town.
One was a black stallion
with fire in its eyes.
It had already thrown four cowboys
when Martha Jane came along.
"You be careful now," they warned her.
"I'll take my chances," she said.
"I'm as stubborn as three mules,
and my kick is worse."

She came up to the horse slowly.

"I know you're just showing off,"
she said softly.

"Everyone can see
how big and strong you are."

The horse snorted.

"I'm just a little thing, though,"
Martha Jane went on.

"And throwing me won't mean much.
But if you let me ride you, you'll make
those rough and tough cowboys
feel even worse."

Well, nobody could ever be sure
whether that horse really understood.
But Martha Jane was the only one
who ever rode him proper.

That horse came in pretty handy too.

One day, Martha Jane was out riding

when she came across an army patrol

fighting for their lives.

Martha Jane didn't wait for a moment.

She swooped in,

pulled the wounded captain

up on her horse,

and rode away with him to safety.

When he recovered,

he took to calling her Calamity Jane.

And the name stuck

like honey on a bear's tongue.

Living in Deadwood

When Calamity Jane was all grown up,
she moved to Deadwood, South Dakota.
This mining town was friendlier
than its name, though not by much.
There she met all kinds
of cowboys and gunfighters
with a few upright folk mixed in.

The most famous was Wild Bill Hickok.
He was tougher than new leather
and didn't smile
but once or twice a year.
Wild Bill had been an army scout
and town marshal.
But he was retired
from those jobs at present.

As a young man,

Bill had once gone eight months

without changing his clothes.

Then one night, while Bill was sleeping,

a bear smelled him and his clothes

a mile away.

It followed the scent right up to Bill

and took a bite out of his leg.

Bill woke up directly.

And before that bear made a meal out of him,

Bill started wrestling.

The bear had his claws, but Bill had a knife.

Over and over they tumbled.

When the dust finally settled,

Bill had himself a new fur coat.

Anyone who could handle a bear

like that was Calamity Jane's

kind of person.

So Bill and Calamity became friends

and traded tales of their famous deeds.

For a real adventure, said Wild Bill,

she should ride for the Pony Express.

The Pony Express was a string of riders

who carried the mail across the frontier.

So Calamity took the job.

Her route was 50 miles

back and forth through the Black Hills.

It was rough country and not just

because of the rocks and ravines.

Outlaws often waited on the trail.

They robbed the riders of money

or packages that they were carrying.

On her third day,
Calamity Jane found three outlaws
waiting for her in a narrow pass.
"Throw down your bags,"
one of them told her.

"Can't do that," she answered.

"I might get a tongue-lashing."

"You could get a lot worse than that,"

said another, flashing his gun.

Before he could even think of shooting,
Calamity Jane had already fired.
Her first bullet hit the outlaw's gun
dead on, going straight up the barrel
and jamming the chamber.
Her next bullet cut the reins
on the second outlaw's horse.

The horse reared up,
throwing its rider to the ground.
"Maybe we'll let you go this once,"
said the third outlaw, backing away.
"Are you sure?" said Calamity.
"Seems like this party
is just getting started."

But the outlaws didn't answer.
They skedaddled out of there so fast
even their dust was left behind.
So Calamity kept on riding,
and nobody bothered her after that.

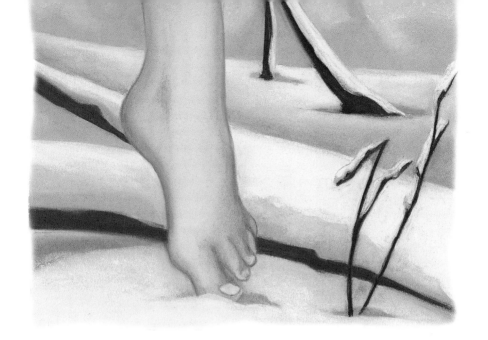

Changing Times

Most people thought Calamity Jane

was tougher than old beef jerky.

She walked barefoot through the snow,

they said.

And she could look into the sun

without blinking.

But Calamity had a softer side too.

She just didn't advertise it much.

One time, the whole town of Deadwood
came down with smallpox.
There was so much itching
and scratching, it sounded like an army
of grasshoppers marching through.
The doctor got sick.
The sheriff felt poorly.
Even the undertaker
hoped nobody would die.
He just wasn't up to burying them.

Almost everyone took to their beds.

But not Calamity Jane.

No one knew why she didn't get sick.

Some folks said her skin was too thick

for the smallpox to get in.

Others figured that even smallpox

wouldn't dare to tangle

with her blood and guts.

Whatever the reason, Calamity Jane
was the one healthy person
who wasn't afraid
to tend to the sick folks.
So she set to nursing them.
It took a few months for the smallpox
to run its course.
Calamity didn't get much sleep.

In one stretch,
she was up for three days straight.
"I had to use broom handles
to prop my eyes open," she said.
"And some didn't last more than
an hour before they snapped in two."
When folks finally recovered,
they wanted to thank her, of course.
But she could only put up
with so much of that.

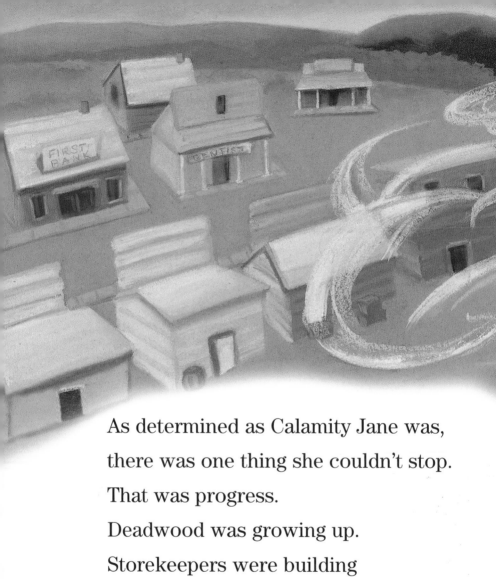

As determined as Calamity Jane was,
there was one thing she couldn't stop.
That was progress.
Deadwood was growing up.
Storekeepers were building
wooden sidewalks
so people didn't have
to walk through the mud.

The Pony Express was gone.

There were no more stagecoaches
to rescue.

In their place was that belching monster
called the railroad.

People were even talking
about putting bathrooms indoors,
but Calamity knew that
was a load of foolishness.
Still, there was no denying
the town had changed.
Now Calamity wasn't about
to get misty over these things.
But she wasn't ready
for a rocking chair just yet.
So when she found herself sitting still
long enough to see a spider spin a web,
she knew it was time to move on.

The whole town turned out
to see her off.
"We'll miss you," said the mayor.
"If we find any trouble,
we'll send for you straight away."
"Fair enough," said Calamity Jane,
"I've always liked trouble."
Then she rode off into the sunset.